For Libby Rose
~*J.W.*

For my patient family
~*N.B.*

122 Fifth Avenue
New York, NY 10011

ISBN-13: 978-1-4351-0874-5 · ISBN-10: 1-4351-0874-4

Printed and bound in Malaysia by Imago

1 3 5 7 9 10 8 6 4 2

Mouse, Look Out!

Judy Waite
illustrated by
Norma Burgin

LITTLE TIGER PRESS
London

The gate no one opened
was rusted up and old.
When the wind blew,
it sometimes creaked and sighed.

And tucked amongst the cracks
of the ivy covered wall,
a little mouse was peeping.

DANGER
EP OUT

Then silent as the sunset,
a shadow came creeping.

MOUSE, LOOK OUT,
THERE'S A CAT ABOUT!

The door no one knocked on
was battered and scratched.
When the wind came calling,
it sometimes bashed and banged.

And through the broken wood,
all raggedy and jagged,
a little mouse was crawling.

Then down the tangled path,
a shadow came creeping.

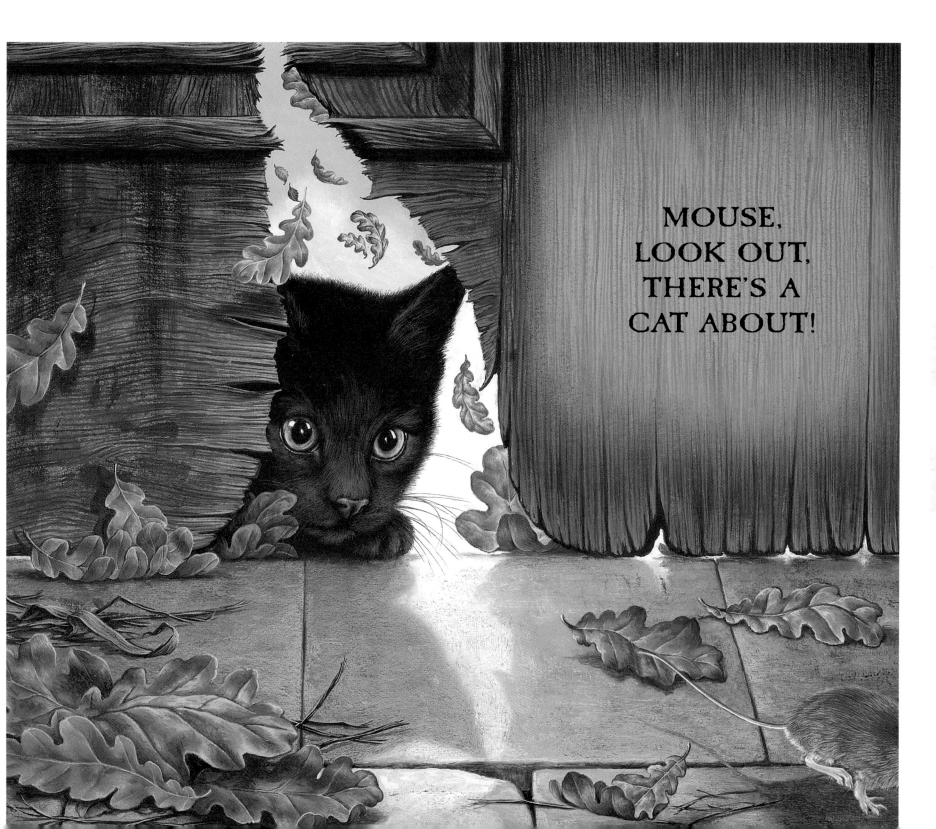

MOUSE,
LOOK OUT,
THERE'S A
CAT ABOUT!

The hallway no one stood in
was musty and dark.
When the wind groaned,
long cobwebs stirred and swayed.
And across the tattered carpet
of frayed and faded patterns,
a little mouse was running.

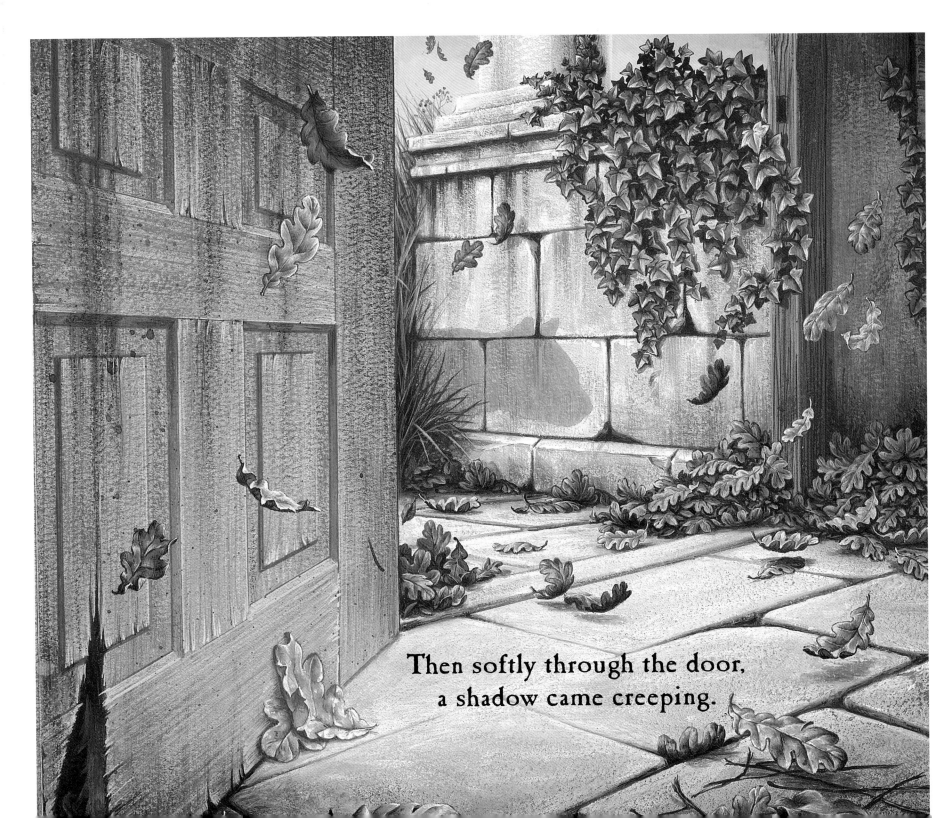

Then softly through the door,
a shadow came creeping.

MOUSE, LOOK OUT,
THERE'S A CAT ABOUT!

The kitchen no one cooked in
was grubby, grey and grimy.
When the wind wailed,
the blinds all crashed and clanked.

And round the piles of pots
and long forgotten cupboards,
a little mouse was sniffing.

Then slowly down the hallway,
a shadow came creeping.

MOUSE, LOOK OUT,
THERE'S A CAT ABOUT!

The staircase no one climbed
stretched upwards in the darkness.
When the wind howled hard,
it echoed with the roar.

And up the giant steps,
with scrabblings and scratchings,
a little mouse was struggling.

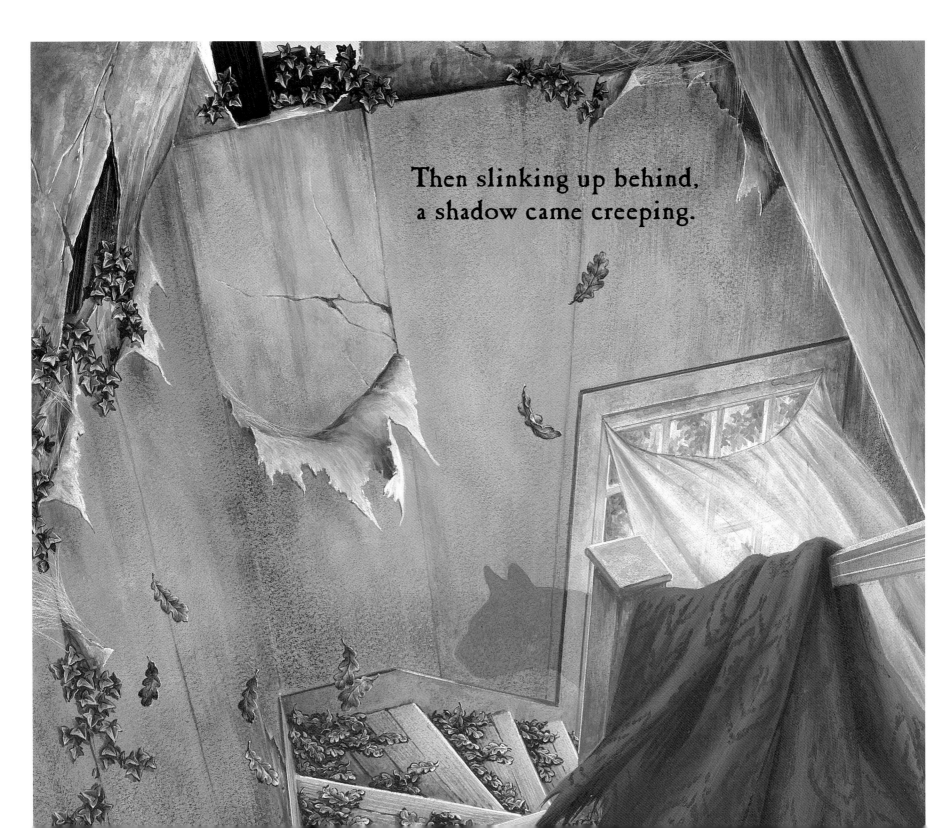

Then slinking up behind,
a shadow came creeping.

MOUSE, LOOK OUT,
THERE'S A CAT ABOUT!

The room no one slept in
was jumbled up with junk.
When the wild wind dropped,
the bed seemed safe and warm.

And in amongst the mess,
inside the torn, worn mattress,
a little mouse was snuggling.
Then through the quiet room,
something came leaping . . .

CAT,
LOOK OUT,
THERE'S A
DOG ABOUT!